MEG'S VEG

for Sam

MEG'S VEG

by Helen Nicoll
and Jan Pieńkowski

PUFFIN BOOKS

It was springtime. Time for Meg
to start her vegetable garden

Meg fetched the muck

Mog dug the earth

Owl raked it smooth

Owl
sowed
peas
and
carrots

Mog
put in
a
pumpkin

Meg
sowed
some
seeds
she
had
found
in
her
cauldron

It was so cold, no seeds grew

Mog made a scarecrow to guard his pumpkin

Meg tried to make the sun shine

Camel's hump
And vulture's eye
Make it bake
And frizzle and fry

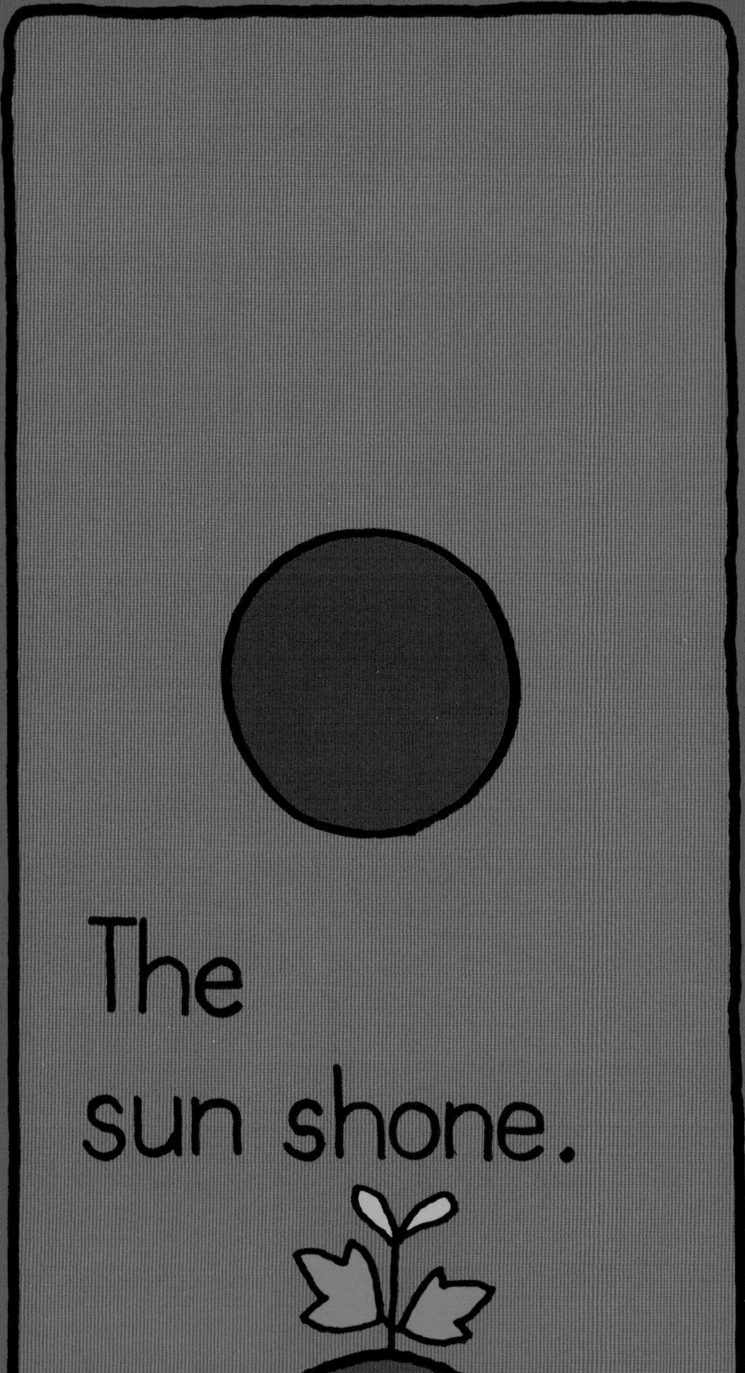
The
sun shone.

It got
hotter

and hotter

and hotter

poor thing it needs a drink
Make it rain! Make it rain!

Splish splosh
All awash
Wellington boots
And mackintosh

The rain came down in sheets

It's raining it's pouring
SPLISH SPLASH SPLOSH

The garden grew like a jungle

These aren't peas

They had

to pull up all the weeds

1..2..3..
HEAVE

POP
Ouch
Meeow
Squawk

They made a huge compost heap

Then
they
had to
stake
the
peas

and thin out the carrots

They had to hoe down the rows

and water the pumpkin

And then,
they
had to
eat
them
all

Goodbye!